ESCAPE

ESCAPE

SOPHIE McKENZIE

Illustrated by
MELANIA BADOSA

Barrington Stoke

Published by Barrington Stoke
An imprint of HarperCollins*Publishers*
1 Robroyston Gate, Glasgow, G33 1JN

www.barringtonstoke.co.uk

HarperCollins*Publishers*
Macken House, 39/40 Mayor Street Upper,
Dublin 1, DO1 C9W8, Ireland

First published in 2026

Text © 2026 Sophie McKenzie
Illustrations © 2026 Melania Badosa
Cover design © 2026 HarperCollins*Publishers* Limited

The moral right of Sophie McKenzie and Melania Badosa to be identified
as the author and illustrator of this work has been asserted in accordance
with the Copyright, Designs and Patents Act, 1988

ISBN 978-0-00-875894-3

10 9 8 7 6 5 4 3 2 1

All rights reserved. No part of this publication may be reproduced, stored in
a retrieval system, or transmitted, in whole or in any part in any form or by any
means, electronic, mechanical, photocopying, recording or otherwise without
the prior permission in writing of the publisher and copyright owners

Without limiting the exclusive rights of any author, contributor or the publisher of
this publication, any unauthorised use of this publication to train generative artificial
intelligence (AI) technologies is expressly prohibited. HarperCollins also exercise
their rights under Article 4(3) of the Digital Single Market Directive 2019/790 and
expressly reserve this publication from the text and data mining exception

A catalogue record for this book is available from the British Library

Printed and bound in India by Replika Press Pvt. Ltd.

This book contains FSC™ certified paper and other controlled
sources to ensure responsible forest management.

For more information visit: www.harpercollins.co.uk/green

For Louisa

CHAPTER 1

Bernice loved the sea and everything that lived in it. She wanted a job looking after sea animals when she left school. Today, she was on a school trip to Eco-Marina, near where she lived. Eco-Marina was a sea-life sanctuary where scientists and vets looked after sick and injured sea creatures.

"Get into groups of three!" ordered Mr Willis, the teacher in charge.

"Hey, Bernice!" said her best friend, Molly. "We're in a group with Rylan. I've already asked him!"

This was not good news. Rylan Alexander was the most annoying boy in their year. Molly had a massive crush on him. Bernice had no idea why.

Mr Willis handed out worksheets. Bernice took one.

"Listen, everyone, please!" the teacher boomed. "You have two hours to find the answers to the questions on your worksheet. You're free to go anywhere you like within the sanctuary." He frowned. "Eco-Marina is not open to the public, and it is a huge privilege for our school to be here today, so you must follow the rules on the top of your worksheet."

Bernice glanced down at the paper as Mr Willis read the rules out loud:

Stay with your group at all times.

**Do not go anywhere marked
out of bounds.**

**Above all, behave!
That means don't go near the animals,
no shouting and no littering.**

Bernice sighed. No way would Rylan stick to those rules, especially the one about behaving.

He was always showing off. And he always thought he was right. Even when he wasn't.

"Boring!" Rylan said softly so Mr Willis couldn't hear.

Rylan had messy blond hair that was always falling over his eyes. He was tall and sporty. Molly thought he was amazing. Bernice thought he was ridiculous.

"Sea animals aren't boring, Rylan," she said.

Rylan made a face. "Whatever, Bernie."

"It's *Bernice*." She frowned.

Rylan gave a shrug. "I was just telling Moll that the sharks are the only thing worth seeing here," he said. "Let's forget everything else."

No way! Bernice couldn't believe what Ryan had just said. "But I really want to see the dolphins they rescued from the aquarium and the injured grey seals in the care pool and the sea turtle recovery area—"

"Like I said – *all really boring!*" Rylan snorted.

Bernice turned to Molly. Up until a few weeks ago, Molly would have been as excited as Bernice to be here, but now all she wanted to do was hang out with Rylan.

"I'd like to see the sharks best too," Molly said. She pointed at the map of the sea sanctuary. The sharks were in Shark Bay, at the far end of Eco-Marina. "Let's go there first, then we'll fit in some other things on the way back. Please, Bernice?"

Bernice sighed again. Mr Willis had insisted they stay in their groups. "OK," she said. "But we *have* to see the rescue dolphins straight after the sharks. I'm not missing them."

"Sure thing," said Rylan with a wink at Molly.

Bernice turned away. She felt more fed up than ever. Then she spotted a notice next to the map.

> **ARE YOU INTERESTED IN WORKING WITH SEA ANIMALS?**
>
> Eco-Marina is offering one lucky young person the chance to work here for the summer.
>
> To apply for this amazing job, you must be aged 16 or 17 and be passionate about marine life!

An email address was underneath. Bernice felt excited. As soon as they'd finished their tour of the sanctuary, she was going to apply for the summer job. If she got it, it would take her a big step closer to her dream of working with sea creatures.

An info sheet on shark myths was pinned next to the ad. Bernice already knew a fair bit about sea creatures from all the internet videos she watched when she was supposed to be doing her homework. She read it quickly. There might be facts here she could use when she applied for the job.

"Let's get to the sharks!" Rylan cried.

Bernice turned around. He and Molly were already walking fast, down to Shark Bay. Bernice felt annoyed, but there was nothing she could do. They were her group; she had to stick with them. She sighed and followed them down the path to Shark Bay.

CHAPTER 2

Molly and Rylan were racing along the path to Shark Bay.

"Hey!" Bernice shouted. "Wait for me!"

She could hear Rylan talking loudly. "They've got basking sharks here," he said. "You know, with those pointy fins that stick up above the water."

"Ooh," Molly gasped. "They sound dangerous."

"Oh, they are," said Rylan. "One sniff of human blood and they'll attack."

For goodness' sake, Bernice thought.

"You're wrong about basking sharks," Bernice said, catching up with Ryan and Molly. "Basking sharks are probably the safest sharks in the world. They're no threat to humans."

Rylan frowned. "No way! Look how big they are! All sharks attack humans. That's the point of them!"

Molly giggled.

"There are lots of sharks here, and they're *all* really dangerous," Rylan went on.

"No, they aren't," insisted Bernice. "Most sharks only attack if humans provoke them, or if someone starts splashing around in front of them so that the sharks think they're food. There's no evidence that they hunt humans on purpose. In fact, humans are far more dangerous to sharks than they are to us."

"Well, *Bernie*, you think that if you want to," Rylan said with a snort, "but I've seen *loads* of movies, and sharks are *killers!*"

He grabbed Molly's hand and dragged her ahead of Bernice along the path. "Come on, Molly – let's go see the assassins of the sea!"

Rylan really was annoying. How could anyone be so stupid and so arrogant? Bernice gritted her teeth.

She caught up with the other two at the edge of Shark Bay. The bay was at the very end of the sanctuary. It was a huge stretch of seawater that made a "C" shape, with the open sea beyond. A path led around the bay. There were railings all along the path, and a sheer drop down to the water.

Molly and Rylan were standing by a big sign which explained that underwater metal netting stopped the sharks from swimming into the open sea.

There was another sign on the railings, much bigger than the one about the underwater netting:

NO SWIMMING or BATHING
Entering the water is strictly prohibited

Rylan pointed to the words. "Look at that, Bernie," he said with a grin. "Why would they be telling us not to go for a swim if the sharks weren't super dangerous?"

"Rylan's got a point," Molly said. "You have to admit that."

"No!" Bernice snapped. "The order not to swim is so people don't disturb the sharks. It's to protect *them*, not us."

"Yeah right," Rylan snorted.

Molly said nothing.

Bernice sighed. It was going to be a long morning.

CHAPTER 3

Bernice stared across the shimmering water. It was very peaceful. She was glad they'd come to Shark Bay now. Maybe they'd even see a shark.

"What stops the sharks swimming out of the bay?" Molly asked.

"Underwater electric fence," Rylan said confidently. "Zap! Take that, sharks!"

Bernice stared at him, feeling shocked. "Zapping them would be cruel," she protested. She pointed to the sign they'd just passed. "Didn't you see that? There *is* a fence, but it's just made of thick wire mesh."

"Where's the fun in that?" Rylan grunted.

Bernice shook her head and gazed out across the calm, still bay. Rylan was *such* a loser. What did Molly see in him?

The path led around the bay, with railings set all along it. Rylan and Molly leaned against the railings and peered across the water.

"I can't see any sharks," Molly said. She looked grumpy.

"Let's go to the underwater observation area," Bernice said. "I'm sure we'll see some sharks there."

"I don't want to see the sharks through a window in a tunnel," groaned Rylan. "Let's stay outside. We can walk to the far end of the bay."

Walking to the end of the bay would take ages. Bernice looked down at the worksheet. There were loads of questions. She read the first three.

1. **Sharks use two thirds of their brain to focus on one sense. Which is it?**

2. **What type of skeleton does a jellyfish have?**

3. **How long can a grey seal hold its breath?**

They weren't going to find the answers to these or any of the other questions by staring out over the empty water. And Bernice needed as much information as possible so as to make her job application as good as it could be.

She checked the time. Nearly half an hour had already passed. The sun had gone in, and there were some dark clouds in the sky. Bernice felt gloomy. She had been really looking forward to today, but it was turning out to be rubbish.

She looked up. Molly and Rylan had already set off along the path. For a moment, Bernice thought she'd leave them to it, but Mr Willis would be angry if she went off on her own. Perhaps, in a few minutes, Molly and Rylan would get tired and turn back.

She shoved the worksheet into her bag and walked quickly after them. The air was much cooler now. Bernice put on her jacket and checked the time. Molly and Rylan had been walking for ten whole minutes and there was still no sign of any sharks. Why didn't they all go and see something else?

It started to rain. The thick, heavy drops pounded down on their heads.

"Oh no!" Molly squealed. She zipped up her jacket and put her bag over her hair.

"Maybe we'll see some sharks now!" said Rylan as he pulled his hood over his head.

"Let's go back," said Bernice. She tugged her own jacket tighter around her. "There's loads to explore, and if we keep walking to the end of the bay, there won't be time to see any of it."

She stared at Molly and Rylan. The other school groups who'd walked this far had headed back to the main part of the sanctuary. The three of them were alone.

Molly hesitated. "It *is* raining," she said to Rylan. "Maybe Bernice is right—"

"No way," said Rylan. He pointed towards the water. "The rain will bring the sharks to the surface – you'll see."

From everything Bernice knew about sharks, she didn't think this was likely. But she didn't say so. She was beginning to work out that the more she challenged Rylan, the more he showed off. Instead, she looked at Molly. The rain was tipping down.

"Don't you want to see the dolphins, Molly?" she asked.

Molly nodded. "Come on, Rylan. Let's go back."

"Just give it another minute." Rylan pointed to the sky, where a patch of blue was showing beyond the dark clouds. "The sun will be out in a second," he said. "And so will the sharks!"

Bernice stopped walking and looked hard at Rylan. "Right, so you're a weather prophet now, Rylan," she said, "as well as a shark expert?"

Rylan stuck out his tongue at her. "Chill out, Bernie."

"Let's wait just one more minute, Bernice," pleaded Molly. "If it doesn't stop raining then, we'll go back."

Bernice gritted her teeth and started counting to sixty as the three of them walked on. Soon the path went inland, away from the sea and behind some high rocks. They couldn't see the bay any longer.

Bernice hung back. "You can't even see the water from here," she grumbled.

"You can here!" called Rylan, who was already round the next bend with Molly.

Bernice hurried after them.

Around the bend, there was a gap in the high rocks, and you could see the bay from the path again, just like Rylan had said.

Bernice peered over the railings to look at the water. There was still no sign of any sharks.

"There! The rain's stopping!" Rylan shouted.

He was right. As the sun came out from behind the clouds, the raindrops dried up. Bernice turned her face to the warm sun.

"Look!" Molly shouted.

There, just in front of them in the water, was the tip of a fin. Bernice peered more closely. Wow! It was a huge, grey-brown basking shark.

It glided through the water, making small side-to-side movements that propelled it slowly forward. Bernice couldn't believe it. She'd never seen a real-life shark before. It was amazing! She took out her phone.

"Let's get closer and grab a selfie!" Rylan cried.

And before Bernice could say a word, he climbed over the railings. She gasped as he stood right on the edge of the bay, just a metre or so from the swimming shark.

CHAPTER 4

Rylan stood on the wrong side of the railings, next to the water, and peered out over Shark Bay.

"Get back here!" Bernice shouted.

Rylan ignored her. "Come on, Molly!" he called. "It's totally safe. The sea is way below us. And the stupid shark can't climb out, ha ha!"

Then Rylan took his phone out of his pocket and started turning to and fro and posing, trying to find the best angle for a photo. The sun vanished behind another cloud.

"Molly!" he shouted again. "Come and take a selfie with me!"

"Can I borrow your mobile, Bernice?" Molly asked. "*Please?* Mine's not charged, and I want to get a picture of me with Rylan."

Bernice stared at her. "Why do you have to do everything Rylan says?"

"Why do you have to be so lame?" Molly said crossly. "It's just one quick photo."

Before Bernice could say anything else, Molly had snatched Bernice's phone and clambered over the railings.

Bernice looked left and right. There were high rocks on all sides of the water. At least they were totally hidden from view here, so nobody else could see Rylan and Molly being so stupid.

"Hey, Rylan!" Molly giggled. "Can you get us *and* the shark in the picture?"

"Stupid shark won't stop moving," said Rylan. He was shifting from side to side with his phone out in front of him. Molly stood next to him and flicked back her hair. She made a photo face, pouting at the phone.

Bernice shook her head. "Of course it won't stop moving," she snorted. "It's a basking shark, and they *can't* stop moving. It's how they breathe."

"Course it is!" muttered Rylan in a sneery way.

"You're such a know-it-all, Bernice!" Molly laughed.

Tears pricked at Bernice's eyes. Molly had stopped being a good friend a few weeks ago, but this felt like the end. Bernice pressed her lips together and tried not to cry.

"I'm going to do a short," Rylan cried. "It'll look sick!" As he switched his phone to video, Molly held out Bernice's mobile in front of her.

"I'll do one too!" Molly took a step back. She was right next to Rylan now.

The large, sleek basking shark was still swimming lazily to and fro just a few metres away.

"Careful!" Bernice shouted.

But it was too late. As Rylan turned, he bumped against Molly's arm. Both of them lost their balance.

And before there was even time to scream, Rylan, Molly and both the phones had fallen into the water.

CHAPTER 5

Bernice stared, horrified as Rylan and Molly splashed about in the bay. Out of nowhere, rain began falling again, pattering on the water.

"Help!" Molly shrieked. She reached up, trying to grab at the edge of the path. But it was no good. The path was too high for her to reach.

"Aaagh!" Rylan yelled. "Shark! *Shark!*"

Molly turned in the water and saw the fin of the basking shark. It was still swimming to and fro just a few metres away.

Then Molly let out a terrible scream. "Look! There's two of them!"

A second fin had joined the first.

Rylan swore. "We're going to *die!*" he yelled.

"It's OK!" Bernice shouted. "They won't hurt you!"

But Rylan and Molly were shrieking and splashing and making too much noise to hear her.

Bernice climbed over the railings. Her stomach was twisting with worry. The water was over a metre below her, but maybe if she reached over and grabbed their hands, they'd be able to climb out.

"Molly! Rylan! Come here!" she yelled.

But they were swimming away. Bernice stared at them. What were they doing? Even stupid Rylan must know they wouldn't be able to outswim a shark. Sharks might move slowly when there was no need to hurry anywhere, but if they wanted, they could be super speedy.

She looked around the bay. She couldn't see a member of staff. She couldn't see anyone. All the other school groups would be back in the dry now.

"Molly!" As Bernice called out again, the rain grew heavier. Huge drops pounded down, making her wet even through her jacket.

She didn't have her phone. Molly had taken it earlier, and now it was at the bottom of the bay. Bernice couldn't call for help. She felt sick, scared and angry.

The rain poured down. Bernice watched as Molly and Rylan swam towards a sea cave. It was set in the rocks just two or three metres away.

"We're going to hide from the sharks in here!" Molly shouted.

Bernice could only just hear her because of the noise of the rain on the water.

"Get help before the sharks eat us!" yelled Rylan.

For goodness' sake. Bernice opened her mouth to yell again that the sharks wouldn't hurt them. But before she could make a sound, Molly and Rylan vanished inside the cave.

CHAPTER 6

Bernice stared at the entrance to the little cave. The rain was heavy, and her jacket was soaked through, but she didn't care. She was the angriest she had ever been in her life.

Molly and Rylan were not only stupid but selfish. If they had listened to her, they wouldn't have fallen in the water and disturbed the beautiful sea creatures in the bay. And they wouldn't have swum into a cave to hide from totally non-dangerous sharks.

Now, here she was, her clothes dripping and damp against her skin and without her phone. Mum was going to be furious that she'd lost it, even though it wasn't her fault. As for Mr Willis ... Bernice didn't want to think about what he'd say to them.

The entrance to the sea cave was just a few metres away. She scanned the water. No sign of any fins. She yelled in the direction of the cave at the top of her voice.

"Molly! Rylan! There aren't any sharks now! You *have* to swim back here. I can help you get out!"

She waited. The rain thundered down. Her hair was so wet it stuck to her head, and water dripped down the back of her collar. Molly and Rylan didn't come out of the cave.

Could they even hear her over the pounding rain? Bernice yelled their names louder. "Swim! Back! Here! *NOW!*" she shrieked.

This time, a small noise came from inside the cave. Bernice frowned. Was that Rylan's voice? She strained to hear.

"Help, Bernice! *Help!*"

It *was* Rylan. Was this a wind-up?

His cry came again. "*Please*, Bernice. *Hurry!* It's Moll—" The rest of his sentence was drowned out by thunder.

There was something in Rylan's voice – and the way he'd called her "Bernice" instead of "Bernie" – that told her he wasn't pranking her.

Something was seriously wrong

She stared at the bay. The sharks had vanished under the surface, and the seawater was churning as the rain battered it. Bernice was already wet through anyway.

Her heart thudding, she slipped off her shoes and jacket, then eased herself down into Shark Bay.

CHAPTER 7

The water in the bay was so cold it made Bernice gasp. Waves splashed against her face, and she could taste salt on her lips.

She swam as hard as she could towards the sea cave. Her wet clothes felt like a weight, dragging at her. She peered into the gloomy cave. Waves slapped at the rocks as she tried to see inside. The cave went a long way back.

"Rylan? Molly?" she called. "Where are you?"

"At the back!" Rylan yelled, his voice echoing off the cave walls.

"Hurry, please!" Molly panted.

Bernice waited a moment. The chill of the water was starting to seep into her bones. After the way they had mucked about earlier, there was no way Bernice could be sure that Molly and Rylan weren't just trying to get her into the cave for a laugh.

If this was a wind-up, she would never speak to either of them again.

Bernice swam along the left-hand side of the cave. Her fingers were numb with cold. A dark shadow loomed up out of the water just ahead.

"Bernice, thank goodness!" The shadow leaned towards her, and she made out Rylan's pale, shivering face.

"What are you doing?" She swam nearer. "Where's Molly?"

"I'm here!" Molly gasped.

Bernice peered down. Molly was almost fully underwater. Rylan was holding up her head, tipping it back so that Molly's nose and mouth were just above the surface.

"What happened?" asked Bernice.

"We swam in to get away from the sharks," Rylan said.

"My foot ... I was on a ledge," Molly spluttered, a small wave splashing over her face. "Now ... I'm stuck."

Rylan's teeth were chattering. "She can't get her foot out," he went on. "I tried to dive down, but when I let go of her head, she goes under the water."

"It's like I ... I'm sinking." Molly sounded worn out and terrified.

Bernice looked out of the sea cave towards the bay. From here, it was just a grey smudge of light. It looked as if the rain had stopped, but the bay was part of the sea. And the sea had tides.

"You're not sinking. The tide's coming in," Bernice said. She tried hard not to show that she was in a panic. The water was already creeping up around Molly's mouth. "I'm going to dive down and free your foot while Rylan holds you up. OK?"

The others nodded. "Hurry!" gasped Molly.

Bernice took a deep breath and dived.

CHAPTER 8

Bernice dived down through the cold, murky water. The salt stung her eyes, but she kept going, following the white of Molly's jeans down to the foot of her left leg.

There. Molly's foot was stuck in a crack in the rock. Bernice tugged at the ankle, but the foot was stuck fast. Bernice felt sick. She made herself focus. Perhaps if she undid Molly's trainer, Molly could wriggle her foot out of it.

Bernice felt around the shoe, her lungs starting to strain for breath. There were two thick strips of Velcro. Quickly, Bernice pulled at them. She really needed to breathe now, but she couldn't stop. She yanked at Molly's foot, twisting and lifting. *There.* It was free.

Lungs burning, Bernice turned and pulled her way back to the surface. Her body felt heavy now, her lungs on fire. She broke through the water and gulped down big mouthfuls of air.

Opposite her, Molly's head rose out of the water.

"Thank you!" she panted.

"Come on!" Rylan cried. "Let's get out of here!"

The three of them swam towards the cave entrance.

"That was close," Molly gasped as she pulled herself through the water. "I— Aaagh!" She let out a terrified squeal.

Bernice saw the fin of a shark swimming in circles just outside the cave.

"Oh no!" Rylan turned to Bernice. "Is that another basking shark?" he spluttered. "You said they were harmless, right?"

Bernice looked at the fin. It was smaller than the one on the shark they'd seen before. She frowned.

"I think we're good," Rylan went on. "It's much smaller than that first shark. Yeah,

just a baby." He looked hopefully at Bernice. "Isn't it?"

Bernice shook her head. "This is a different shark altogether. A shortfin mako."

"What does that mean?" Molly asked.

"If its smaller, then surely it's slower and less dangerous?" Rylan added.

"It doesn't work like that." Bernice slowed her movements in the water. "Mako sharks are really fast and powerful ... and they're not like basking sharks. They have been known to attack humans."

CHAPTER 9

"Oh no!" Molly's voice rose in panic.

"After all that, we're still going to be eaten by a shark!" Rylan cried, splashing in the water. He sounded very scared.

"I don't want to die!" Molly wailed.

"Shut up, both of you!" Bernice snapped. "The poor shark won't attack us unless we upset it or provoke it."

Rylan and Molly stared at her.

"Speak in whispers," Bernice ordered. "And stop splashing. Small, gentle strokes only."

Molly and Rylan slowed right down until they were swimming just enough to stay afloat.

"Now what?" Rylan whispered.

"We swim slowly and carefully out of the cave and past the shark."

Bernice set off. Molly and Rylan swam after her.

Bright sunlight was now shining down on the bay outside. In a few strokes, the shortfin mako was close. So close that Bernice could see its smooth, gleaming skin just under the water.

It was beautiful, she thought. Why couldn't people see that sharks were just part of the natural world? They were not evil monsters like in the stories and films.

As she watched, the mako swam even closer. Bernice stopped swimming, knowing that the less she moved around, the better. Behind her, she could hear the others slowing right down too.

For a long moment, she and the mako shark stared at each other. And then, as if it thought the three humans in the water were boring, the shark turned and swam off at top speed.

Bernice blew out her breath, super relieved, then started swimming again.

She swam quickly back to where Rylan and Molly had fallen into the water. Her shoes and jacket were still there on the path above their heads. Rylan, who had the longest arms, reached up, but he could only just get his fingertips to the very edge of the path.

"You'll have to push me up!" he cried.

Bernice grabbed him round the middle, and with Molly on the other side they heaved him high enough so he could haul himself out of the water. Bernice sank back, worn out, the waves splashing at her face.

Rylan was already reaching down for Molly. Bernice helped push her up, out of the water, then the other two grabbed Bernice's arms, and with their help she managed to scramble out of the bay.

She clambered over the railings, then lay panting on the path. The air was cold, even though the sun was now shining brightly, and Bernice shivered. Seawater poured out of her clothes.

"Bernice Charles!" Mr Willis's shout broke through the silence.

Bernice jumped up.

"Swimming is totally forbidden!" A man in the green sweatshirt with the Eco-Marina logo stood beside their teacher. He looked shocked.

"W ... w ... w ... we ... we ... re ... n't ..." Bernice tried to say, but her teeth were chattering too much. She huddled next to Molly and Rylan, all three of them shivering in the chill air.

Mr Willis drew himself up. "You three are in *serious* trouble!"

CHAPTER 10

Bernice sat in the Eco-Marina admin office beside Molly and Rylan. The sanctuary staff had wrapped them in blankets and given them Eco-Marina sweatshirts to change into as well as a cup of hot, sweet tea.

A nurse had checked Molly's ankle was OK. She was nice. But everyone else who'd come over had given them a cross look, as if to say how stupid they'd been.

Bernice was really depressed. She'd missed out on exploring Eco-Marina and seeing dolphins in real life, and she'd blown any chance of working at the sanctuary. Instead, she'd probably get a detention at school and be grounded by her mum. She'd lost her phone too.

Mr Willis strode in and sat in a chair in front of them. He looked very serious. A woman came in with him. She stood by the window. She was wearing a badge with her name and job title: *Dana Rogers, HR and office manager.*

"What happened?" barked Mr Willis. "How did you end up in the water?"

Bernice looked at the ground. She didn't know what to say. She waited for Rylan to tell Mr Willis the whole thing had been a bit of fun. Molly would back him up, of course.

"*Well?*" Mr Willis went on.

"It was our fault," Molly said softly. "Me and Rylan."

Bernice couldn't believe it. That was not what she had expected. She looked over at the others. Rylan was glaring at Molly, who jutted out her chin and stared back at him. Bernice held her breath.

"Rylan?" Mr Willis asked.

"I guess what Molly says is true," Rylan said with a sigh. "I climbed over the railings and got Molly to join me. We were doing a video, but we slipped and fell in the water."

Mr Willis nodded slowly. "What about you, Bernice?"

She opened her mouth to explain how she'd ended up in Shark Bay, but before she could speak, Molly was talking again.

"Bernice only came in to save me. Rylan and I were scared of the sharks, and we ended up in a little cave, and I got my foot trapped, and if Bernice hadn't swum in and got me out, I'd have drowned." Molly stopped for a second. "That's true, isn't it, Rylan?"

"I wasn't scared," Rylan protested. "But, yes, Bernice did get Molly out." He looked over at Bernice. "She saved us from the shark too."

Mr Willis frowned. "Saved you from a shark?"

Rylan gave a shrug. "If you must know, Mr Willis, I had a few ideas about sharks which weren't exactly, um, correct, but Bernice knew exactly what to do. She told us that we just needed to stay calm and not upset it, and she was right."

Bernice looked down at her lap.

"Please don't punish her," Molly went on. "We needed her help, and she came, even though I'd grabbed her phone off her, and … and it got lost in the water."

"Which I suppose meant she couldn't call for help," Mr Willis said slowly.

"That's right." Rylan took a deep breath. "If there are any detentions going around, I don't think Bernice should have to do them. It wasn't her fault she ended up in the water."

"Or lost her phone," Molly added. "I'm going to explain about that to your mum too, Bernice." She turned and smiled at her friend.

Bernice didn't know what to say. She thought she might cry.

"I see," said Mr Willis. "And what do you have to say for yourself, Bernice?"

Everyone stared at her.

"Molly and Rylan got into trouble, so I had to try to help," Bernice began.

"Yes, I can see that." Mr Willis looked across the room at Dana from Eco-Marina. "Well, this is a very different story from what we thought happened."

Dana nodded. "It sounds like you understand quite a bit about sharks, Bernice?"

Bernice sat up. "I do and … and I hope what happened today won't count against me because I'd really, really like to apply for the summer job. I saw the notice earlier, and it would be, like, my *dream* to work here."

"Ooh, yes, Bernice would be *perfect* for that," Molly said. "She knows loads about sea animals. Not just sharks."

"She's good at standing up for herself too," added Rylan.

"I see." Dana smiled. "Well, Bernice, I suggest you apply as soon as you can. I'll look out for your email."

"Thank you," Bernice said. "Er, there is one more thing. Is there any chance I could …

Is there time to look around the sanctuary before we go back to school?"

Dana and Mr Willis looked at each other.

"Please let her," Molly said. "Thanks to me and Rylan, Bernice hasn't seen anything apart from the sharks. I know she *really* wanted to visit the dolphins. They're her favourites."

Bernice smiled. She was very surprised that Molly remembered how much she loved dolphins.

"Is that right, Bernice?" Mr Willis asked.

Bernice nodded. "Yes, they are."

"Well, there should be just enough time for you to visit the rescue dolphins before we leave." Mr Willis turned to Molly and Rylan. "You two can wait on the coach."

"Yes, sir," said Molly and Rylan.

"Thank you," said Bernice.

Mr Willis and Dana left. Bernice ran her fingers through her hair. It was almost dry now. She turned to the others.

"Thanks for ... for what you said," she stammered.

"No worries! Say hello to the fish for us, Bernie!" Rylan winked.

Rylan was still getting it all wrong. But Bernice didn't say anything this time.

"Actually, dolphins are mammals, Rylan," Molly said. Then she winked at Bernice.

Rylan shrugged and walked over to the vending machine.

"Shall I save you a seat on the coach next to me, Bernice?" Molly asked.

Bernice stared at her. Molly had sat with Rylan on the way here.

"Don't you want to sit next to Mr Lush?" she asked, looking at Rylan.

Molly shook her head. "I'd rather hang out with my bestie for a bit and hear about the dolphins." She grinned hopefully. "Is that OK?"

"Sure." Bernice grinned back, then hurried outside into the sunshine.

THIS WORKSHEET WAS COMPLETED BY:

Bernice Charles

1. **Sharks use two thirds of their brain to focus on one sense. Which is it?**

   That's the sense of smell. Sharks are really sensitive to smells as it helps them identify whether a scent comes from a predator that they want to avoid or their dinner!

2. **What type of skeleton does a jellyfish have?**

   Jellyfish are invertebrates and have an ~~enda~~ ~~endi~~ endoskeleton.

3. **How long can a grey seal hold its breath?**

   Like for a whole hour or more! They can even sleep underwater!

Eco-Marina – Summer Job

From: **Dana Simmons**
(DanaSimmons@HightopEcomarina.org)

To: **Bernice Charles**
(BerniceCharles@heartanimalmail.com)

Hi Bernice.

I'm pleased to inform you that you have been successful in your application for the summer job here at Eco-Marina. Congratulations! We already knew how much you understand about sharks from your school visit last month (!), but my colleagues and I were also very impressed with your knowledge of other sea creatures, as well as the commitment to preserving and caring for marine life that you showed in your letter of submission. More details are enclosed in the attached document, but please let me know if you have any questions. We look forward to welcoming you to the team in a few weeks.

Best wishes,
Dana

Dana Simmons | HR and office manager

Eco – Marina
SEA-LIFE SANCTUARY

Our books are tested
for children and young people by
children and young people.

Thanks to everyone who consulted on
a manuscript for their time and effort in
helping us to make our books better
for our readers.